froglets

ANIMAL OLYMPICS

Hippo's High Dive

by Damian Harvey and Andrew Painter

W

FRANKLIN WATTS

LONDON • SYDNEY

Franklin Watts
First Published in Great Britain in 2016
by the Watts Publishing Group

ISBN 978 1 4451 4776 5 (hbk)
ISBN 978 1 4451 4778 9 (pbk)
ISBN 978 1 4451 4777 2 (library ebook)

Series Editor: Melanie Palmer
Series Advisor: Catherine Glavina
Series Designer: Peter Scoulding

Printed in China

Franklin Watts
An imprint of
Hachette Children's Group
Part of The Watts Publishing Group
Carmelite House
50 Victoria Embankment
London EC4Y 0DZ

An Hachette UK company.
www.hachette.co.uk

www.franklinwatts.co.uk

Hippo loved diving,
but her last dive had
been a disaster.

All the water had

splashed out ...

Snake's pencil dive had been perfect.

Tiger's tumble had been terrific.

Even Alligator's armstand
had been amazing.

Now it was
Hippo's turn.

Hippo would have to do something really special to win. She'd have to dive off the very top board.

11

Hippo was about to climb up, but then she stopped. "I'm sure I've forgotten something," she said.

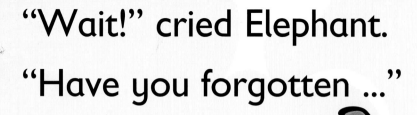

"Wait!" cried Elephant.
"Have you forgotten ..."

14

"My goggles!" said Hippo.
"That's it. Thank you,
Elephant."

"I can't dive without these!"
Hippo put on her goggles
and got ready to climb up.

"Wait!" cried Rhino,
"you've forgotten ..."

"My diving hat!" said Hippo. "That's it! Thank you, Rhino."

"I can't dive without my lucky hat!"

Hippo put on her hat
and off she went.

Up she went, to the very, very top. Then she looked down and remembered ...

"Hippos hate heights!"

She quivered and quaked.

Then she shivered and slipped.

Hippo twisted and turned.

She flipped and she rolled.

Then landed in the water
with a ...

27

It was perfect and everyone cheered!

Puzzle 1

Put these pictures in the correct order.
Now tell the story in your own words.
How short can you make the story?

Puzzle 2

forgetful   jealous

scared

upset   pleased

happy

Choose the words which best describe the characters. Can you think of any more? Pretend to be one of the characters!

Answers

Puzzle 1

The correct order is:

1b, 2f, 3e, 4a, 5d, 6c

Puzzle 2

The correct words are forgetful, scared.

The incorrect word is jealous.

The correct words are happy, pleased.

The incorrect word is upset.

Look out for more stories:

Robbie's Robot
ISBN 978 1 4451 3950 0 (HB)

The Green Machines
ISBN 978 1 4451 3954 8 (HB)

The Cowboy Kid
ISBN 978 1 4451 3946 3 (HB)

Dani's Dinosaur
ISBN 978 1 4451 3942 5 (HB)

Gerald's Busy Day
ISBN 978 1 4451 3934 0 (HB)

Billy and the Wizard
ISBN 978 0 7496 7985 9

The Frog Prince and the Kitten
ISBN 978 1 4451 1620 4

Bill's Scary Backpack
ISBN 978 0 7496 9468 5

Bill's Silly Hat
ISBN 978 1 4451 1617 4

Little Joe's Boat Race
ISBN 978 0 7496 9467 8

Little Joe's Horse Race
ISBN 978 1 4451 1619 8

Felix, Puss in Boots
ISBN 978 1 4451 1621 1

The Animals' Football Cup
ISBN 978 0 7496 9477 7

The Animals' Football Camp
ISBN 978 1 4451 1616 7

The Animals' Football Final
ISBN 978 1 4451 3879 4

That Noise!
ISBN 978 0 7496 9479 1

Cheeky Monkey's Big Race
ISBN 978 1 4451 1618 1

For details of all our titles go to: www.franklinwatts.co.uk